This Book Belongs to:

_____

For Henry.

Maisie Mae
From Sunnyside Street

By Stephanie Jane Markham • Pictures by Graziella Miligi

First Printing, 2021

I'm Maisie Mae
from Sunnyside Street.
I'll show you my dreams,
come along and see!

I'd like to live inside a tree with
Princess Rebecca, just her and me.
We'd sing like birds and
drink honeyed tea.

We'd run so fast,
our feet would grow.
We'd race a snail and
go soooo slowww.

Then, climb the sky!
Jump the clouds!
Slide down rainbows,
laughing loud!

I'd dance the jig in big red shoes.
I'd fly a kite with kangaroos.
Bouncing high into the sky!

So high I'd bounce up to planet Mars, and make my playground in the stars, with seven sparkly sisters skipping rope.

I could be a raincloud,
caught up in a storm.
I could ride atop a lightning bolt
and watch the raindrops swarm!

I'd sneak up on the faeries, around the faerie ring.
I'd drink from all the flowers and they would give me wings.

And then my best friend, Duncan,
would bring his unicorn!
She's magical, does ballet, and
has a purple horn.

We'll gallop on our unicorn,
her name is Letty Lou.

Around the town
and upside down.

We'll drop in on the zoo.

Our unicorn, our Letty Lou,
would talk like zebras do.
And make friends with the
animals, who'll show us
round the zoo.

Giraffes would
race us!
Lions would
chase us!

The Mama
Gorilla would
try to
embrace us!

Then, off to Ann and Emma's house. They're our friends. And twins!

They have a garden big as a park.
With a roundabout! And swings!
Simon and Sabrina will
come along to play.
Simon loves to read his books.
Sabrina sings all day.

We'll run through all the daffodils.

And throw stones by the stream.

We say goodbye and off we fly.
There's still time left to dream!

When Mommy calls to come inside, I'll race to earth at rocket speed. I'll surf in on the ocean's tide.

Then, search for hidden treasure on a pirate ship joy ride. Starboard, onward, home!

I'll cartwheel down my garden
path with Sebastien, the gnome.

After my adventures,
I'll tell my Mom my tales of
unicorns and shooting stars
and how to ride the snails.

Then snuggled up in my bed,
I'll dream of all the fun I had
and tomorrow...

...do it all again!

CPSIA information can be obtained
at www.ICGtesting.com
Printed in the USA
LVHW070913151021
700536LV00005B/54

9 780578 910321